I've broken the maths curse.

I can solve any problem.

And life is just great until science class, when

Mr Newton says,

"**YOU KNOW**, you can think of almost everything as a science experiment..."

Wednesday morning at 7:15.

It takes me 10 minutes to get dressed,
15 minutes to eat my breakfast,
and 1 minute to brush my teeth.
My bus leaves at 8:00.

What time will I be ready?

 **7:41**

NO PROBLEM.

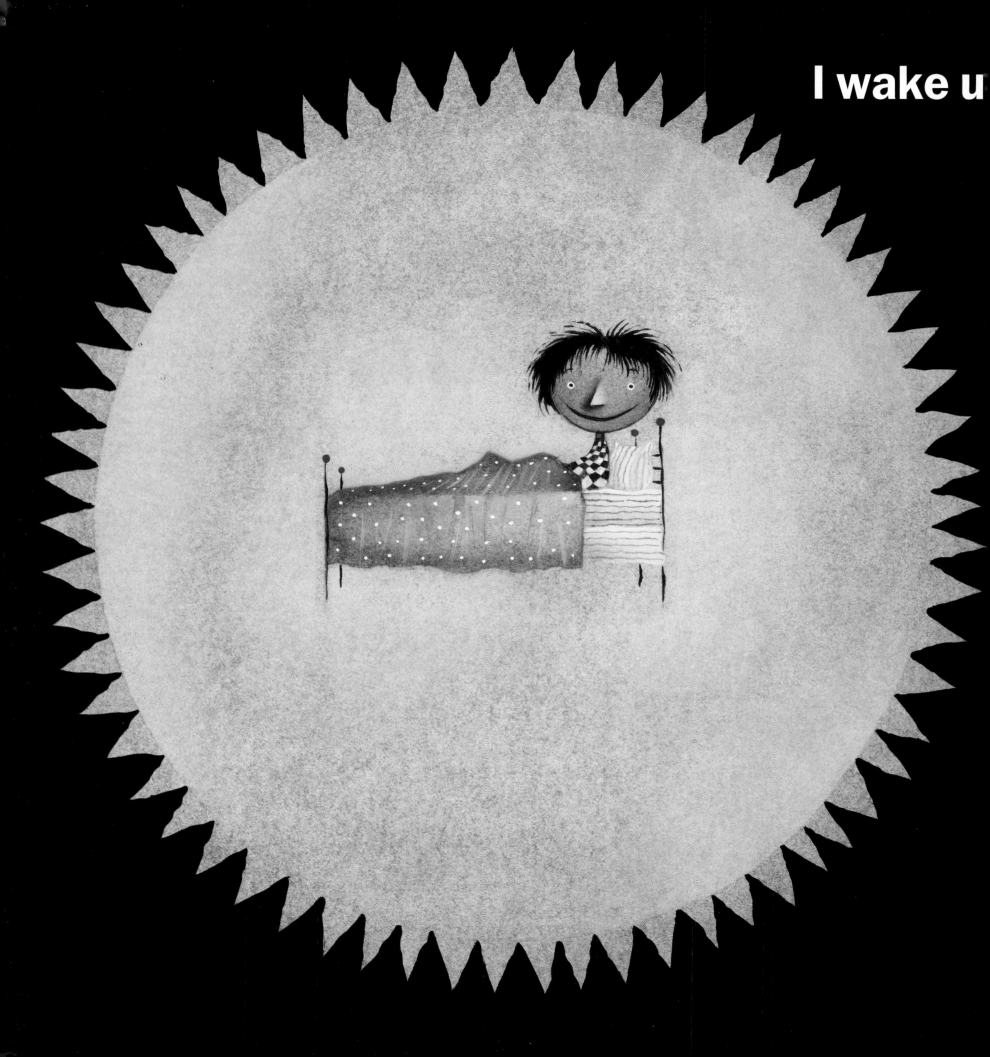

I wake u

I'M FREE.

I put the hole on the wall and jump out.

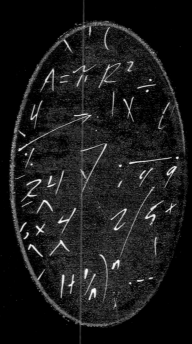

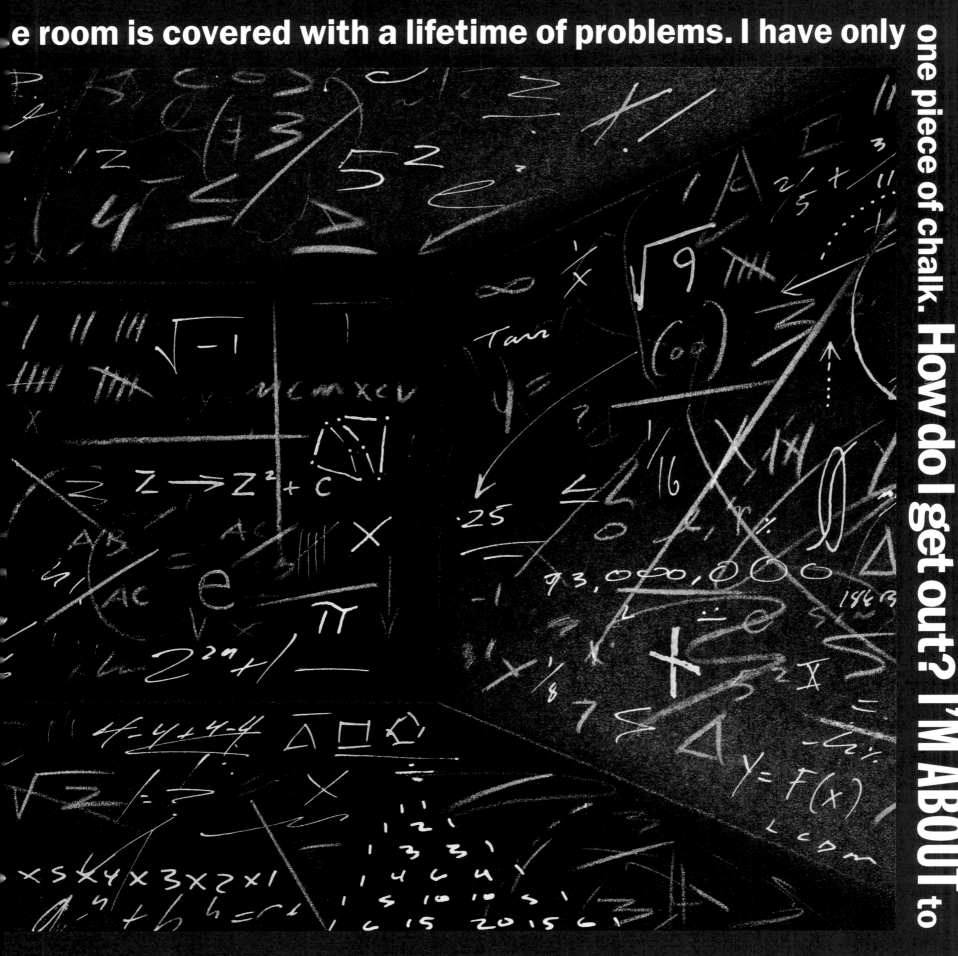

e room is covered with a lifetime of problems. I have only one piece of chalk. How do I get out? I'M ABOUT to give up and die, when the answer to my problem comes to m

halves together. One half plus one half equals one whole.

I am now a raving maths lunatic.

What if this keeps up for a whole year?

How many minutes of maths madness would that be?

"What's your problem?" says my sister.

"365 days x 24 hours x 60 minutes," I snarl.

Dinner brings no relief.

While passing the mashed potatoes,

Mum says, "What your father says is false."

Dad helps himself to some potatoes and says,

"What your mother says is true."

I think about that for a minute.

If what Mum says is true, then what Dad says is false.

But if what Dad says is false, then what Mum says isn't true.

And if what Mum says isn't true, then what Dad says isn't false.

But that can't be true because he says that what

Mum says is true, and she says that what he says is false.

Can that be true?

I think about that. Then I think about it some more.

Then I think I'd better go to bed.

I undo 8 buttons plus 2 shoelaces.

I subtract 2 shoes.

I multiply times 2 socks and divide by 3 pillows to get 5 sheep,

remainder 1, which is all I need to count before I fall asleep.

Then the problems really begin.

I stagger out of school.

I'm a maths zombie now.
I have to find something to break this maths curse.
I decide to try chocolate.
My favourite candy bar is usually 50¢.

But guess what?

Today it's on sale for 50% off:

$$\frac{-B \pm \sqrt{B^2 - 4AC}}{2A}$$

Where **A** = the number of letters in your first name, **B** = your age, and **C** = your shoe size

I decide to buy liquorice instead.

I pull out my money.

I have a $5 bill, a $1 bill, a quarter, and a penny. George Washington is on both the quarter and the $1 bill. Abraham Lincoln is on both the penny and the $5 bill.

✔ **SO WHICH IS TRUE:**
a. 1 Washington equals 25 Lincolns.
b. 5 Washingtons equal 1 Lincoln.
c. 1 Washington equals 100 Lincolns.
d. 1 Lincoln equals 20 Washingtons.

Don't forget to show your work.

EXTRA CREDIT: How do you think Thomas Jefferson feels about all of this?

We are just about to go home when Rebecca remembers the special birthday cupcakes her mum made.

There are 24 KIDS in the class.
Rebecca has 24 CUPCAKES.

✗ So what's the problem?

Rebecca wants Mrs Fibonacci to have a cupcake, too.

Everyone is going crazy trying to figure out
what fraction of a cupcake each person will get.

I'm the first to figure out the answer.

I raise my hand and tell Mrs Fibonacci
I'm allergic to cupcakes.

EVERYONE (24) believes me
and gets ONE (1) cupcake.
NO ONE (0) has to figure out fractions.

ENGLISH is a word problem:

If mail + box = mailbox:

❶ Does lipstick – stick = lip?

❷ Does tunafish + tunafish = fournafish?

PHYS. ED. is a sports problem:

In 1919, Babe Ruth hit 29 home runs, batted .322, and made $40,000.

In 1991, the average major league baseball player hit 15 home runs, batted .275, and made $840,000.

☛ CIRCLE THE CORRECT ANSWER:

Babe Ruth < The average modern baseball player

Babe Ruth > The average modern baseball player

Babe Ruth = The average modern baseball player

In the afternoon, every subject is a problem.

SOCIAL STUDIES

is a geography problem:

The Mississippi River is about 4,000 kilometres long.

An M&M is about 1 centimetre long.

There are 100 centimetres in a metre, and 1,000 metres in a kilometre.

① Estimate how many M&Ms it would take to measure the length of the Mississippi River.

② Estimate how many M&Ms you would eat if you had to measure the Mississippi River with M&Ms.

BONUS: Can you spell Mississippi without any M&Ms?

Unfortunately for me,
LUNCH is pizza and apple pie.
Each pizza is cut into 8 equal slices.
Each pie is cut into 6 equal slices.
And you know what that means:
fractions.

① **If I want 2 slices of pizza should I ask for:**

a. 1/8
b. 2/8
c. 2 slices of pizza

② **What is another way to say 1/2 of an apple pie?**

a. 2/6
b. 3/6
c. la moitié d'une tarte aux pommes

③ **Which tastes greater?**

a. 1/2 a pizza
b. 1/2 an apple pie

We haven't studied fractions yet,
so I take 12 carrot sticks 3 at a time
and eat them 2 at a time.

THE WHOLE morning is
one problem after another.
There are **24 kids** in my class.
I just know someone is going to
bring in cupcakes to share.
We sit in **4 rows** with **6 desks** in each row.

What if Mrs Fibonacci rearranges
the desks to make 6 rows?
8 rows?   3 rows?   2 rows?

I COUNT the 24 kids in our
class again, this time by 2s.

Jake scratches his paper
with one finger.
➤ **How many fingers
are in our class?**
Casey pulls Eric's ear.
➤ **How many ears
are in our class?**
The new girl, Kelly,
sticks her tongue out at me.
➤ **How many tongues
are in our class?**

I'M about to really lose it,
when the lunch bell rings.

6 5 2 5 BUS

DECEMBER

OCT   NOV   DEC

Mrs Fibonacci has this **CHART** of what month everyone's birthday is in:

① Which month has the most birthdays?

② Which month has the fewest?

③ Why doesn't February have a *w*?

④ Don't you think this chart looks sort of like a row of buildings?

⑤ Do you ever look at clouds and think they look like something else?

⑥ What does this inkblot look like to you?

I TRY to get on the bus without thinking about anything, but there are **5 KIDS** already on the bus, **5 KIDS** get on at my stop, **5 MORE** get on at the next stop, and **5 MORE** get on at the last stop.

✔ **TRUE OR FALSE:**
What is the bus driver's name?

JAN FEB MAR APR MAY JUN JUL AUG SE

I TAKE the milk out for my cereal and wonder:

① How many quarts in a gallon?

② How many pints in a quart?

③ How many inches in a foot?

④ How many feet in a yard?

⑤ How many yards in a neighbourhood? How many inches in a pint? How many feet in my shoes?

I don't even bother to take out the cereal. I don't want to know how many flakes in a bowl.

Mrs Fibonacci has obviously put a

MATHS CURSE

on me. Everything I look at or think about has become a maths problem.

t 7:15. It takes me 10 minutes to get dressed, 15 minutes to eat my breakfast, and 1 minute to brush my teeth.

SUDDENLY, it's a problem:

❶ If my bus leaves at 8:00, will I make it on time?

❷ How many minutes in 1 hour?

❸ How many teeth in 1 mouth?

I look in my closet, and the problems get worse:

I have 1 white shirt, 3 blue shirts, 3 striped shirts, and that 1 ugly plaid shirt my Uncle Zeno sent me.

❶ How many shirts is that altogether?

❷ How many shirts would I have if I threw away that awful plaid shirt?

❸ When will Uncle Zeno quit sending me such ugly shirts?

I'M GETTING a little worried.
Everything seems to be a problem.

Mrs Fibonacci says,

"**YOU KNOW**, you can think
of almost everything
as a maths problem."

On Tuesday I start having problems.

ON MONDAY in maths clas

If the sum of my nieces and nephews equals 15, and their product equals 54, and I have more nephews than nieces, HOW MANY NEPHEWS AND HOW MANY NIECES IS THIS BOOK DEDICATED TO?

—J.S.

If I divide the number of years my dad was an accountant (30) by the number of years I needed help with my maths (30), I get one (1) dedication: FOR DAD (THE C.P. A.)

—L. S.

PUFFIN

Published by the Penguin Group
Penguin Books Ltd, 27 Wrights Lane, London W8 5TZ, England
Penguin Putnam Inc., 375 Hudson Street, New York, New York 10014, USA
Penguin Books Australia Ltd, Ringwood, Victoria, Australia
Penguin Books Canada Ltd, 10 Alcorn Avenue, Toronto, Ontario, Canada M4V 3B2
Penguin Books (NZ) Ltd, 182–190 Wairau Road, Auckland 10, New Zealand

Penguin Books Ltd, Registered Offices: Harmondsworth, Middlesex, England

First published in the USA by Viking 1995
Published in Great Britain by Viking 1995
1 3 5 7 9 10 8 6 4 2
Published in Puffin Books 1998
1 3 5 7 9 10 8 6 4 2

Made and printed in Singapore

British Library Cataloguing in Publication Data
A CIP catalogue record for this book is available from the British Library

ISBN 0–140–56381–4 Paperback

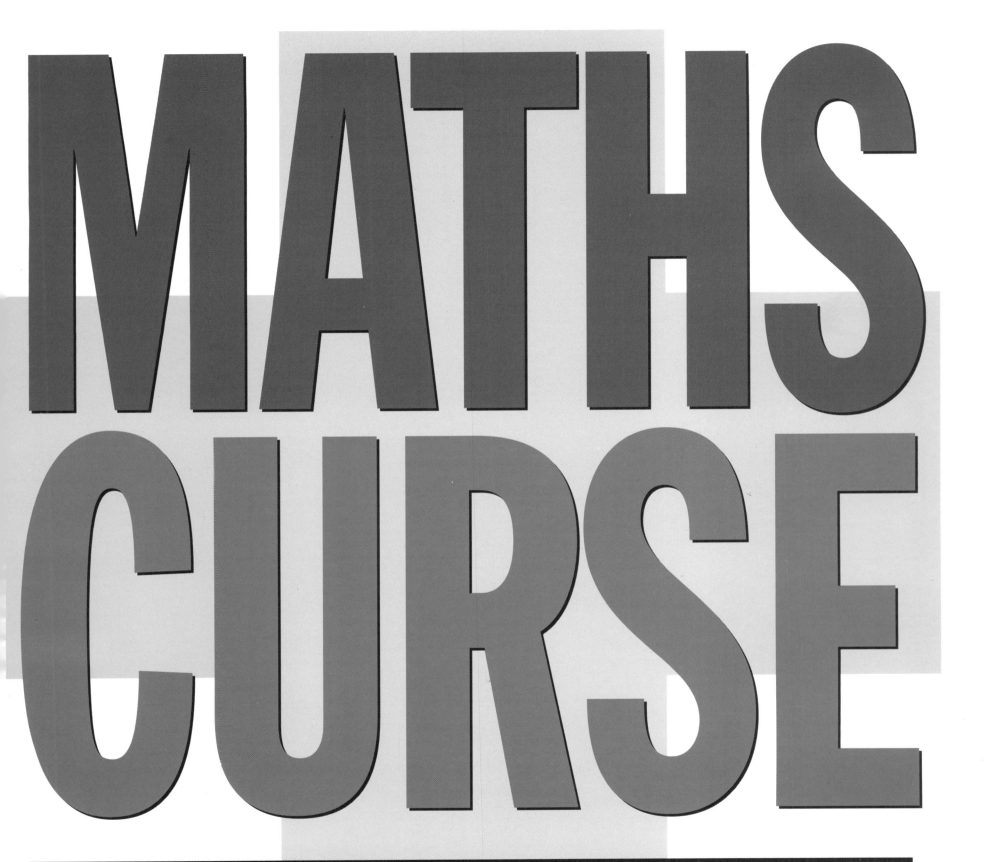

MATHS CURSE

JON SCIESZKA AND LANE SMITH

PUFFIN BOOKS